THANKS TO:
God for his direction in all my books.

My grandchildren Belinda, Matthew,
James, Reagan, Tatum, Nikita, and Lukas
who are the joys in my life.

All rights reserved. No parts in this book may be reproduced, stored in a retrieval system, or transmitted in any form by any means, electronic, chemical or otherwise, without the author's prior written permission.

Published and illustrated by Melinda Sutherland.

Copyright © 2022 Melinda Sutherland

ISBN: 9798373086646

TABLE OF CONTENTS

The Tatumator.. 1

Reagan's Ball... 19

The Magic of the Treehouse.. 35

Lukas the Inventor Goes on an Adventure.. 55

AUTHOR'S NOTES

Never in my wildest dreams did I think the stories I made up for my grandchildren would be published. Not only were they fun to do, but the preschool teacher in me became part of the stories.

It is my prayer you embrace the innocence of children by allowing them to simply dream and play as children should do.

The Tatumator

On Monday, Tatum's mommy was vacuuming the living room.

She tried to move the couch so she could vacuum under it, but it was too heavy.

Tatum flew into the room and said,
"I can move it for you, because
I am the Tatumator!"

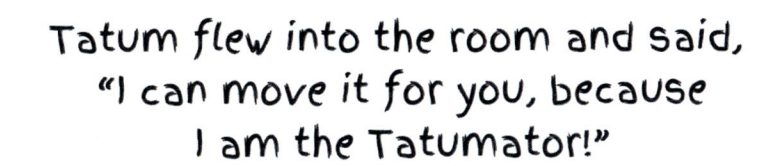

Tatum moved the couch
using only her pinky finger.

"Thank you," said her mommy.
"You are welcome," said Tatum.

OFF SHE FLEW

On Tuesday, Tatum's daddy
was working on his truck.

A wrench fell under it. No matter how much
he tried, he could not reach the wrench.

Tatum flew to the truck and said, "I can pick up the truck for you, and then you can get your wrench, because I am the Tatumator!"

Tatum picked up the truck with her little toe while her daddy got the wrench.

"Thank you," said her daddy.
"You are welcome," said Tatum.

OFF SHE FLEW

On Wednesday, Tatum's sister Belinda went for a walk.

Belinda couldn't see anything because it was raining so hard.

Tatum flew to her and said, "I can block the rain for you because, I am the Tatumator!"

Tatum turned her body into a giant umbrella that protected Belinda.

"Thank you," said Belinda.
"You are welcome," said Tatum.

OFF SHE FLEW

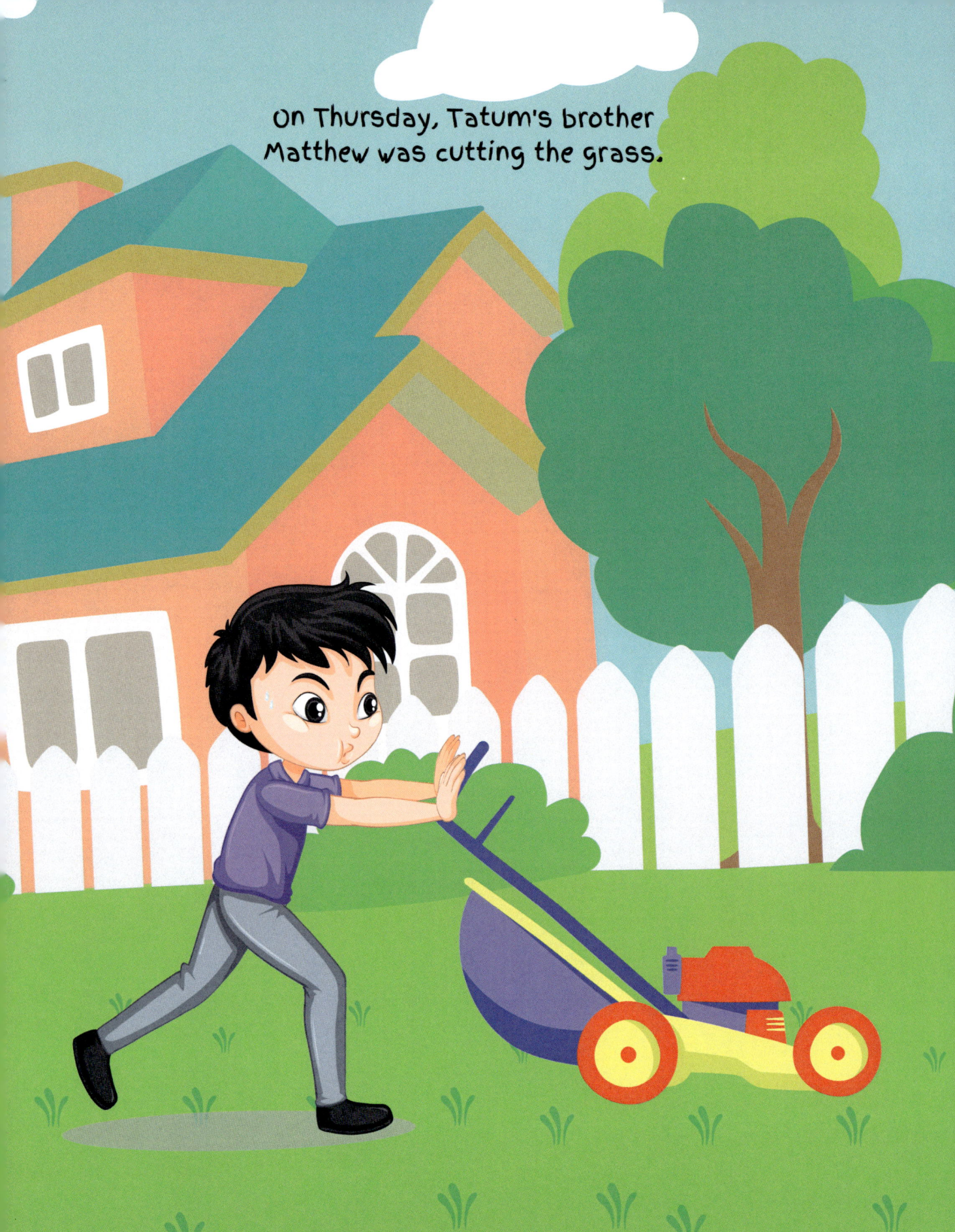

On Thursday, Tatum's brother Matthew was cutting the grass.

For some reason the lawnmower stopped, and it would no longer start.

Tatum flew down to him and said,
"I can help you cut the grass, because
I am the Tatumator!"

Tatum got on her hands and told Matthew to hold
her legs and push her. As he was pushing her,
Tatum started to eat the grass like a lawnmower.

"Thank you," said Matthew.
"You are welcome," said Tatum.

OFF SHE FLEW

On Friday, Tatum's twin sister Reagan was riding her bike.

Out of nowhere a big boulder blocked her way.

Tatum flew down and said," I can move that boulder for you because, I am the Tatumator."

She hit the boulder with her fist and made an opening.

"Thank you," said Reagan.
"You are welcome," said Tatum.

OFF SHE FLEW

On Saturday, cousins Nikita, Lukas, and James were playing in the swimming pool.

All of a sudden a whirlpool appeared.

Tatum flew to them and said,
"I can save you because,
I am the Tatumator!"

Tatum took a deep breath and blew
the whirlpool up to the sky.

"Thank you," said cousins
Nikita, Lukas, and James.

"You are welcome," said Tatum.

OFF SHE FLEW

On Sunday, Tatum's family was leaving for church when a big giant monster blocked the door.

"There will be NO church for you today!" yelled the giant. What were they to do?

Tatum turned to her family and said, "I need a little more help."

"I will call on my friend, God."

Tatum told all her family to hold hands and pray for God to remove the giant.

God made the giant disappear.

On Monday, Tatum continued her journey to help others.

After all, nothing could stop her, because she knew where her strength came from

...her very good friend, God.

WHAT DO YOU THINK....

Can you name the days of the week?

How did The Tatumator help her mommy?

How did The Tatumator help her daddy?

How did The Tatumator help Reagan?

How did The Tatumator help Belinda?

How did The Tatumator Help Matthew?

How did The Tatumator and her family stop the monster?

Did you see the small monster?

Who can you help?

What would your superhero name be?

What is your superpower?

WOW - YOU ARE AMAZING!

What is the next story?

Reagan's Ball

One autumn morning, Reagan was looking at the different color leaves on a tree.

She noticed one leaf on the tree looked like her favorite ball.

She wanted to play with it, so she looked for her ball.

She looked under her dolls.

She looked in her toy box.

She looked behind her stuffed animals.

But she could not find her ball.

Reagan needed help.

She asked her twin sister, Tatum to help find her ball.

They looked under the dogs.

They looked in the fish tank.

They looked behind the iguana.

But they could not find Reagan's ball.

Reagan needed more help.

She asked her older sister and brother, Belinda and Matthew, if they could help her find her ball.

They looked under the couch.

They looked in the game cabinet.

They looked behind the televison.

But they could not find Reagan's ball.

23

Reagan needed more help.

She asked her mommy and daddy if they could help her find her ball.

They looked under the table.

They looked in the refrigerator.

They looked behind the microwave,

But they could not find Reagan's ball.

Reagan had an idea.

She called her Uncle Damon, Aunt Lena, cousins Nikita and Lukas to see if she left her ball at their house.

They looked under the computer.

They looked in the filing cabinet.

They looked behind the printer.

But they could not find Reagan's ball.

25

Reagan had another idea.

She called her Uncle Dustin, Aunt Maki, and Cousin James to see if she left her ball at their house.

They looked under the swings.

They looked in the playhouse.

They looked behind the sandbox.

But they could not find Reagan's ball.

Reagan thought she would never find her ball.

Later that day she and Tatum were going
to Nana and Poppie's house to stay the night.

When they arrived, Reagan ran to them and said,
"Nana, Poppie, I lost my ball. Did I leave it here?"

They looked under
the apple tree.

They looked in
the barn.

They looked behind
the pile of leaves.

But they could not find
Reagan's ball.

27

It was getting dark. Nana told Reagan they would look again tomorrow.

Tatum said, "Sissy, when we say our prayers tonight, we can ask God to help us find your ball."

Reagan said, "OK."

Nana could see that Reagan was sad. She had an idea to help Reagan feel a little better.

"Who wants to go outside and sit on the porch?" asked Nana.

"I do," said Reagan.

"I do," said Tatum.

"Sure"

"Will you play your guitar?"

"Will you tell us a story?"

"I'm coming too"

Reagan, Tatum, and Poppie were dancing while Nana played her guitar and sang funny songs.

Reagan almost forgot about her ball because she was having so much fun.

All of a sudden, Reagan stopped dancing and yelled, "My ball! My ball! I found my ball! Nana, Poppie come see my ball."

Nana and Poppie ran over to Reagan who was pointing to her ball.

At first they couldn't find it, but then they followed Reagan's finger.

"Oh, what a magnificent ball you have! I'm so glad you found it. We would have never looked for it there," said Poppie.

It was big, round, white, and so bright
that it lit up the whole sky.

Reagan, Tatum, Nana, and Poppie
tried to jump up and touch it,
but it was too far away.

Reagan and Tatum stood behind
Nana and Poppie and played
hide-go-seek from Reagan's ball.

Reagan and Tatum were tired, so they climbed onto Nana's lap, and laid their heads on her shoulders.

Reagan was about to close her eyes when she remembered she needed to do something. She slowly raised her head, looked into the sky, and whispered,

"Thank you, God, for finding my ball. I love you."

Then she fell asleep.

WHAT DO YOU THINK....

Can you name three prepositions?

Did you see any pictures that represent three countries?

What were those countries?

Who did Reagan ask her to help find her ball?

Did Reagan find her ball?

Where was she when she found her ball?

What was her ball?

What is season is used for this story?

WOW...YOU ARE AWESOME!

The Magic of the Treehouse

Nikita loved to play in the treehouse his daddy and Poppie built for him and his brother, Lukas.

When he played in it, he could be anything he wanted, and go anywhere he wanted.

One day he was playing with his
LEGO bricks in his treehouse
when he heard someone yelling,

HELP!
HELP!

He said the magic words,

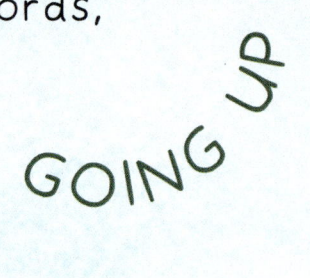

GOING UP

then he turned into a treehouse.

Now, he was ten feet tall and could see who was yelling for help.

It was a little girl one mile away who
had fallen off her bike and
in the path of a fast-moving car.

Nikita blocked the car, picked her up, and safely placed her on the side of the road.

The little girl said, "Thank you, Mr. Treehouse." Nikita said, "You are welcome. Now you are strong enough to help someone else who is in danger."

Then he went home turning back into Nikita.

Later that day, he was reading a book inside the treehouse when he heard someone yelling,

STOP IT! STOP IT!

He said the magic words,

GOING UP

then he turned into a treehouse.

Now he was twelve feet tall and could see who was yelling.

It was a little boy two miles away who was being picked on by some bigger boys.

They were pushing him around and calling him names.

Nikita stood in front of the little boy and told the other boys, "Being a bully doesn't make you cool, it only makes you drool."

The boys left with their tongues hanging out and green snot coming from their noses.

45

The little boy said, "Thank you, Mr. Treehouse."
Nikita said, "You are welcome. Now you are strong enough to help someone else who might be teased."

Then he went home turning back into Nikita.

The next day Nikita was playing basketball in the treehouse when he heard someone crying.

He said the magic words,

GOING UP

then he turned into a treehouse.

Now he was fourteen feet tall and could see who was crying.

It was a little boy three miles away,
who was sad because no one
would played with him.

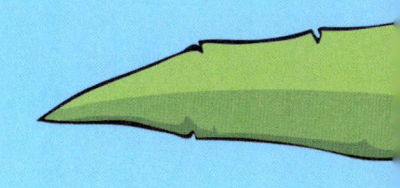

Nikita took a big jump, landing next to him. He asked the little boy, "Would you like to play with me?" "Yes!" said the little boy.

The little boy and Nikita played all day long with airplanes, boats, and pretended to be pirates.

Nikita told the little boy it was time for him to go home. The little boy said, "Thank you, Mr. Treehouse." Nikita said, "You are welcome. Now you are strong enough to help someone else who is alone." Then he went home, turning back into Nikita.

That night at supper, Nikita was eating his favorite meal of macaroni and cheese.

Nikita's mommy and daddy asked him about his day. He said, "Oh not much happening. God and I played in my treehouse."

His mommy and daddy smiled at each other, for they knew whenever God and Nikita were together...
there was magic.

52

WHAT DO YOU THINK....

How did the Treehouse help the little girl?

Have you ever been scared?

How did the Treehouse help the boy who was being teased?

Has anyone teased you?

How did the Treehouse help the boy who felt alone?

Have you ever felt alone?

How can you help others who feel the way you do?

What measurements were used in this story?

What games or toys were in the Treehouse?

Who was the "magic" in Nikita's life?

What does empathy mean?

WOW...YOU ARE AN OUTSTANDING FRIEND!

What is the
next story?

Lukas the Inventer Goes on an Adventure

Lukas was very creative with paper, clips, staples, and anything he found in a junk drawer.

To Lukas it wasn't junk, because when he put them together, he made inventions that took him on adventures.

Lukas' mommy gave him one hundred paper towel rolls.

He made a race track that went all around his house..

His daddy gave him two hundred sheets of bubblewrap.

He made a space station that was taller than the trees in his backyard.

His brother, Nikita, gave him three hundred PVC pipes, and he made the longest slide ever.

When he was done, he climbed to the top and gave himself a big push. He went up, down, and all around.

Finally, he landed in Bonfield, Illinois, at his Nana and Poppie's house, which is eighty-five miles away. Nana and Poppie felt a big wind and heard a thud. They looked up, and there was Lukas.
They ran over to him and gave him a hug.

"How did you get here?"
"I made a slide from my house to yours."
"Well, aren't you clever! You must be hungry from your trip."
"Yes! Do you have any macaroni and cheese?"
"Of course. I always have macaroni and cheese for my grandchildren."

Lukas ate four bowls of macaroni and cheese.

After his snack, Lukas wanted to make more inventions. He and Poppie went to the barn to see what there was for him to use. He saw boards, tools, nails, tires, wood glue, just to name a few things.

Lukas drew up a plan for an obstacle course. Nana and Poppie watched him build it all afternoon.

61

The obstacle course was literally out of this world.
It went all the way to the moon.
Lukas, Nana, and Poppie played on it for hours.
They climbed, jumped, swam, crawled and ran.

No one wanted to stop but it was late
and Lukas was hungry. He ate two more
bowls of macaroni and cheese along with
some cucumbers.

After supper, Lukas helped Nana
make some monkey bread for tomorrow.

Monkey bread is great for inventors.

63

It was time for bed. Lukas liked to sleep on the air mattress. Poppie filled up the air mattress while Lukas got a shower.

Lukas wore Poppie's t-shirt when he stayed the night, because it was big on him.

Just before Nana tucked Lukas into bed, she told him she too had an invention.

"What is it?" asked Lukas.

Nana left the room and then returned with her invention.

"I call it, Nana's Cuddling Blanket."

67

"I LOVE your invention."

Lukas placed his blanket on the floor, even though it was his favorite, so he and Nana could cuddle.

Nana's Cuddling Blanket

While they were cuddling Nana and Lukas prayed to God, thanking him for the wonderful day he gave to all of them.

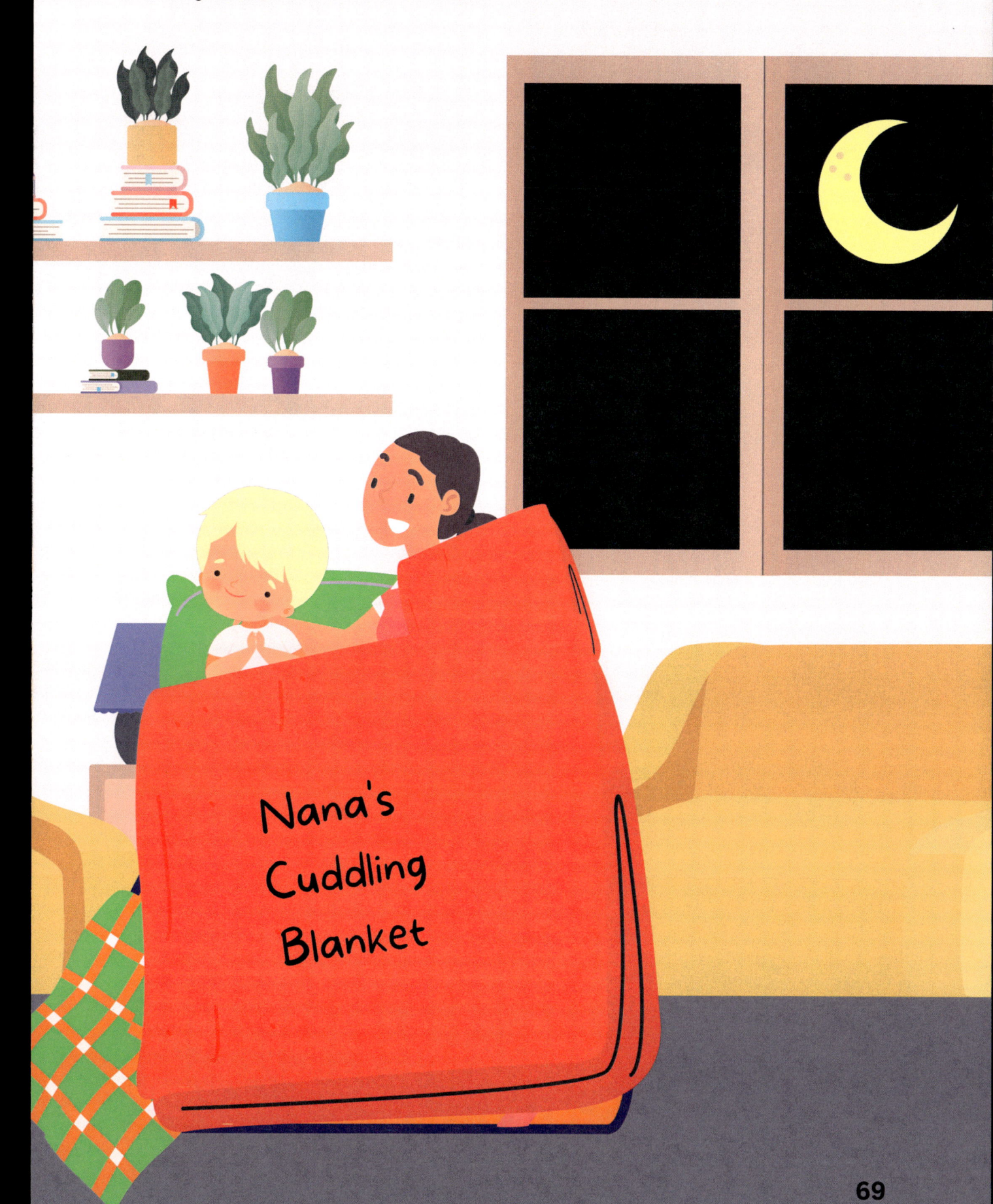

Nana's Cuddling Blanket

When Lukas fell asleep, Nana covered him with his favorite blanket, leaving him to dream about the inventions he will create tomorrow.

WHAT DO YOU THINK....

What is imagination?

What is an invention?

Have you ever invented anything?

What is an adventure?

What would be your favorite adventure?

How many bowls of macaroni and cheese did Lukas eat?

What is your favorite food?

Who did Lukas thank for his wonderful day?

Do you have a favorite blanket?

WOW...I LOVE THE WAY YOU THINK!

Now, you write your own story

Now, you can draw your own story

Made in the USA
Columbia, SC
05 August 2023

ce9ad7f4-bd4e-4d0d-959f-44552e059602R04